YUKI

LUIS

JADA

AWAN

THE

A
SEEK
&
FIND
BOOK

L S T

COUSINS

b.b. cronin

VIKING

Grandad is in the park looking through a photo album.

"Who's that?" ask Esmé and Tate.

"That's Yuki, Jada, Awan, and Luis," says Grandad. "They're your long-lost cousins."

"Let's go find them!" say Esmé and Tate.

Grandad agrees to go with them.

They will need to take a boat, a train, a plane, and even a camel for the journey.

Off they go!

First they take a boat.

This is where Yuki lives. Can you find her?

They all jump aboard a train and travel over a wobbly bridge.

Can you see Awan anywhere?

Next they strap themselves into a very small plane.

This is where Luis lives. Can you see him down below?

To find Jada, they will need a camel to travel across the sand.

Can you see her in the town or walking about?

At last all the cousins are together!

Time to play while Grandad takes a nap after all that traveling.

When Grandad wakes up, he gathers everyone together for a photo for the family album.

"Say cheese!"

Grandad, Esmé, and Tate
are getting ready to go home.

But wait!

They've lost some equipment
along the way. They'll have to retrace
their steps. All the cousins agree
to help—will you, too?

The desert is where Grandad lost his goggles.

Can you help him find them?

Esmé's canteen and Tate's whistle fell out of the plane here.

Can you see where they landed?

This is where they lost their compass, their telescope, and Esmé's sailor hat.

Are they still here?

When they passed here before, Grandad lost their rope and one of his flip-flops!

Can you help him find them again?

At last, everything is found . . .

and their journey takes them back to the park near Grandad's house.

Lost no more!

For Brenda, Denise, and Kendra

———

VIKING

An imprint of Penguin Random House LLC, New York

First published in the United States of America by Viking,

an imprint of Penguin Random House LLC, 2019

Visit us online at penguinrandomhouse.com

LIBRARY OF CONGRESS CATALOGING-IN-PUBLICATION DATA IS AVAILABLE.

ISBN 9780451479082

1 3 5 7 9 10 8 6 4 2

Manufactured in China   Set in Brandon Text

Book design by Mark Melnick

The artwork for this book was rendered with acrylics on paper.